Here's what kids, parents, and teachers have to say to Ron Roy, author of the A to Z Mysteries series:

"I like Dink the best because he never gives up, and he keeps going till he solves the mystery."—Matthew R.

"I'm going to read all of your books! I love your cool descriptions!"—Ashley M.

"I like your books a lot because they give you something to think about!"—Nicole C.

"My third-grade students are now hooked on A to Z Mysteries! Thank you for sharing your talents with children and helping to instill in them a love for reading."—Carolyn R.

To Judson Waack
—R.R.

To Danny Dingo
—J.S.G.

ISBN 0-439-51097-X

Text copyright © 2001 by Ron Roy.
Illustrations copyright © 2001 by John Steven Gurney.
All rights reserved. Published by Scholastic Inc.,
557 Broadway, New York, NY 10012, by arrangement with
Random House Children's Books, a division of Random House, Inc.

24 23 22 21 20 19 18 17 16 15 14   8 9 10/0

Printed in the U.S.A.   40

First Scholastic printing, January 2003

A to Z Mysteries

The Ninth Nugget

by Ron Roy

illustrated by
John Steven Gurney

SCHOLASTIC INC.

New York Toronto London Auckland Sydney
Mexico City New Delhi Hong Kong Buenos Aires

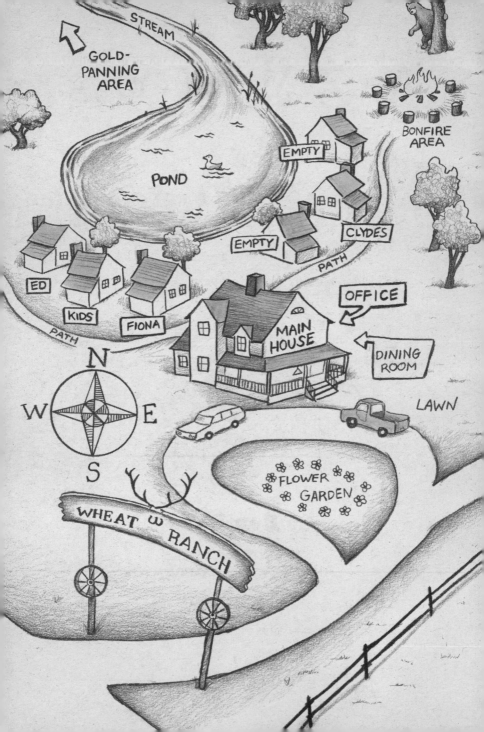

CHAPTER 1

Dink, Josh, and Ruth Rose watched the small airplane rise into the late afternoon sky. They'd just arrived in Bozeman, Montana, for a week's vacation at the Western Wheat dude ranch.

As the kids waited outside the airport for their ride, the sky turned purple. The sun slipped slowly behind the mountains.

"What time is it?" Josh asked. "They said someone would pick us up at five o'clock."

Ruth Rose checked her watch. "It's twenty past," she said.

Dink shielded his eyes against the setting sun. "This might be him," he said.

A dusty station wagon pulled up and stopped. A lanky, smiling guy swung out of the driver's seat. "Are you the kids from Connecticut?" he asked.

Dink nodded. "Are you from Wheat Ranch?"

"You betcha, and welcome to Montana!" the man said. "Sorry I'm late. I'm Jud Wheat."

"I'm Dink, and these are my friends Josh and Ruth Rose," Dink said.

Jud was long-legged and looked about twenty years old. He wore jeans, a western shirt, and scuffed cowboy boots.

"Let me get your stuff," Jud said. He grabbed the kids' backpacks and slung

them into the car through a rear window.

"Hop in and let's ride!" he said.

Ruth Rose and Josh rode up front with Jud. Dink sat behind them with the backpacks, a jumble of harnesses, and a saddle.

"What's that smell?" Josh asked.

Jud laughed. "Some of it's horse, some of it's leather, and the rest is me," he said as he pulled onto the main road.

Only a few other cars and trucks

shared the country road. Through his window, Dink saw plenty of flat land and millions of cows behind neat fences.

"You kids looking forward to riding horses this week?" Jud asked.

"Um, I never rode a horse before," Josh said.

"No problem," Jud said. "Most of our guests haven't. I'll show you all you need to know."

"What do you do at the ranch?" Ruth Rose asked Jud.

"A little of everything, miss," he answered. "My folks own the place, and I grew up there. I was supposed to go back to college this fall, but I have to stay on to help out. The ranch isn't earning much money these days."

"What are you going to college for?" asked Dink.

"I want to be a teacher," Jud said.

"I'd rather spend my days with kids than cows."

Jud pulled up in front of a gas station. "Gotta fill up," he said, stepping out of the car. "I'll just be a minute."

The kids watched as Jud pumped gas into the wagon. Then he loped toward the cashier's window, reaching into his back pocket for his wallet.

"I hope he brings back a few candy bars," Josh said. "I'm starving."

Dink laughed. "After eating about twenty bags of peanuts on the plane?"

Jud stomped back to the car and flung himself into the driver's seat.

"Can you beat that?" he said. "I go into my wallet to pay, and it's totally empty! I'm almost positive I had two twenties in there this afternoon."

Jud shook his head, then grinned. "Well, good thing I had my credit card. Otherwise, we'd be walking!"

Jud drove through more country-side. Dink had never seen so much land! He rolled down his window and felt a hot, dry breeze.

"Look, a hawk!" Josh suddenly yelled.

"He's looking for a nice fat mouse for his supper," Jud said.

Just then Josh's stomach let out a loud growl.

"Someone else is hungry," Jud said, grinning. "We'll be there in a few minutes. How'd you kids happen to pick our dude ranch?"

"We didn't pick it," Dink answered. "A friend of ours gave us this trip as a gift."

Jud grinned into the rearview mirror. "Nice friend," he said.

"His lottery ticket was stolen, and we got it back for him," Ruth Rose explained.

"You mean the ticket was a winner?" asked Jud.

"Yeah," Josh added. "He got seven million bucks!"

Jud whistled. "Seven *thousand* bucks would help the ranch," he said. Minutes later, he turned through a gate into a dirt driveway. A sign hanging over the gate said WHEAT RANCH.

Straight ahead was a red barn and corral. To the left, Dink saw a large white house. Behind it was a pond surrounded by trees and cabins. Ducks and chickens pecked in the grass bordering the driveway.

"This is so beautiful!" Ruth Rose said. "Can I feed the chickens?"

"Sure can, missy," Jud said. He stopped in front of the house.

On the porch sat a man and a woman in two wooden rocking chairs. The man had white hair and looked like an older version of Jud. The woman had black hair turning gray. They both wore boots, jeans, and flannel shirts.

Their tanned faces were covered with smile wrinkles.

"Those are my folks," Jud said. "Everyone calls 'em Ma and Pa."

Jud's parents hurried down the porch steps. "Welcome to Wheat Ranch!" Ma Wheat said. "You must be Dink, Josh, and Ruth Rose."

"Howdy!" said Pa Wheat.

Just then the screen door banged open. A stout woman wearing a backwards baseball cap strode onto the porch. Over her jeans and western shirt, she wore a long white apron.

"And that's Lulu, the best cook in Montana," Jud said as he dumped the kids' backpacks onto the porch.

Lulu smiled at the kids. "They feed you anything on the plane?" she asked.

"Just peanuts," Josh said. "I'm starving!"

"Supper will be ready in fifteen

minutes. Listen for the bell," Lulu said, pointing at an iron triangle hanging from the porch roof.

"I'll take you to your cabin," a deep voice said.

Dink, Josh, and Ruth Rose whipped around. A man had walked up behind them. Wild hair poked out from under a sweat-stained cowboy hat. His skin looked like wrinkled leather.

"I'm Thumbs," the man said. As he reached for the kids' backpacks, Dink saw that one of the man's thumbs was missing.

CHAPTER 2

The kids followed Thumbs down to a narrow path lined with stones. The path led to three small cabins. Behind the cabins, the sun sparkled off the pond.

Dink noticed other cabins farther along the path. "Who's in those?" he asked.

"They're all empty 'cept one," Thumbs grumbled. He stopped in front of the middle cabin.

"This here's yours. There's a lady in that one," Thumbs said, nodding at the cabin to their right. "Some New York feller in the other. Married couple got one of those across the pond."

They were log cabins with chimneys and narrow front porches. There were windows on the sides and in front, where they framed the door.

"Ma Wheat'll give you extra blankets if it turns cold," Thumbs said, clumping up the steps with the backpacks. "You'll find towels in the bathroom."

He nodded at the kids, then clumped off the porch and headed back along the path.

"That guy creeps me out," Josh said. "What do you think happened to his thumb?"

"Maybe a bear bit it off," Dink said, winking at Ruth Rose.

"Could've been a mountain lion," Ruth Rose added, trying not to laugh.

Josh snorted. "Don't try to scare

me," he said. "There's nothing out here but chickens and ducks."

The kids carried their packs into the cabin. A set of bunk beds stood against the far wall, and a single bed was opposite the bunks.

A stone fireplace nestled between the bunk beds and a small bathroom. The only other furnishings were a braided rug, a few chairs, and a table.

"I want to live here forever!" Ruth Rose said. She tossed her backpack on the single bed and looked out her window at the barn.

"I've got upper," Josh said, slinging his pack onto the top bunk.

Dink set his pack on the bunk beneath it as a loud clanging came from the main house.

"Food at last!" Josh said. They ran out of the cabin, nearly colliding with a skinny, bearded man.

"Whoa," the man said, smiling. "No

need to rush. There's plenty of food. You must be the newcomers."

"We just got here," Dink said.

"I'm Ed Getz," the man said. "I came in yesterday from New York." He wiggled his fingers at the kids. "I'm a magician. I'm trying to be an actor, but there's not much work."

Ed Getz had long arms, tapered hands, and thin fingers.

"Cool!" Josh said. "Can you do tricks?"

Ed nodded. "I'll show you some later."

They walked to the main house, then into the dining room. A moose head hung over a wide fireplace. Lassos, spurs, saddle blankets, and bridles decorated the walls.

In front of the fireplace stood a long table and benches. Jud, Thumbs, and three others were already seated. Lulu was placing food on the table.

Ma and Pa Wheat came out of the

kitchen. Ma said, "Hi, kids, take a seat."

Pa tapped a spoon against a glass. "Say howdy to Dink, Josh, and Ruth Rose from Connecticut," he said.

A woman wearing a western shirt and jeans said, "Hello, I'm Fiona Nippit."

"And we're Seth and Bonnie Clyde," said a man sitting next to a pretty woman with long blond hair.

Lulu bustled out of the kitchen carrying a heavy tray of food. "Eat while it's hot!" she said. "What you don't eat now is leftovers tomorrow!"

Everyone began passing platters of fried chicken, mashed potatoes, and steaming vegetables.

With twelve people at the table, it got pretty noisy. The kids learned that Fiona was a nurse from Chicago. The Clydes had just gotten married in Florida and decided to spend their honeymoon at a dude ranch.

Only Thumbs didn't join in the dinner table chatter. While everyone else talked, he just ate.

For dessert, Lulu served apple pie with ice cream on top. By the end of the meal, they were all rubbing their stomachs.

Pa stood up. "It's almost dark. Jud'll build us a bonfire out back. And unless I miss my guess, Thumbs will tell you about the grizzly bear that roams these parts."

Josh shot a look at Thumbs. "Are there *really* grizzlies here?" he asked.

For an answer, Thumbs winked and held up his hand with the missing thumb.

Everyone helped carry stuff into the kitchen. When the table was cleared off, the kids went outside and walked down the path. They found Jud and Thumbs arranging firewood inside a circle of tree stumps.

It had grown almost completely dark. Dink saw a few fireflies in the bushes near the pond.

"Have a seat," Jud told the kids, motioning toward the stumps. They were joined by Fiona, Ed, and the Clydes.

Thumbs struck a match on his belt buckle. He knelt and lit some dry pine needles under the branches, and soon the wood caught.

The flames cast each face around the fire into shadow.

"Is this great or what?" Josh said. "Man, I wish I could stay here longer than a week."

"Me too," Dink said.

Then Ma, Pa, and Lulu came outside. "Got something to tell us, Thumbs?" Pa asked.

Everyone looked at Thumbs. The reflection from the flames made his eyes appear red under his hat brim. He began to speak in a hoarse whisper.

"I'll never forget that night," Thumbs said. "It was a dry summer. There was a lightning storm, and one of the strikes caused a fire. The woods in the hills began to burn. We was sittin' here, just like now. Suddenly, a bear cub came a-runnin' out of the trees. It

was a young'un, just a bitty thing. You could tell it had been burned. It was whimpering, like in pain. We caught the cub, took it inside. Lulu put some butter on the burns."

Thumbs paused. The only sound was wood crackling in the fire.

Dink glanced over at Josh, sitting next to Ruth Rose. Josh's mouth and eyes were wide open.

"What happened to the cub?" Ruth Rose asked.

Thumbs's red eyes turned to Ruth Rose. "Next morning, we took the poor critter to the vet's office," he continued. "When the little thing was all healed up, the vet sent it to a zoo someplace in California."

"Good!" Josh said.

Thumbs swung his gaze back at Josh. "Bad," he said. "The momma grizzly came later that night. She tore through here, howling for her young'un. Probably weighed seven hundred pounds, that grizzly did. Smashed cabin doors, ripped a hole in the barn, sent us all a-hidin' down in Lulu's root cellar."

"D-did she ever come back?" Josh asked.

Thumbs let out a laugh that was more like a cackle. "Sonny, that grizzly pays us a visit at least two, three times every summer. She tears through here like a hairy tornado, destroyin' nearly everythin' in her path."

Thumbs looked at his thumbless hand. "That poor momma wants her baby back. It's been two years now, and she still comes around lookin' for it."

Thumbs placed the thumbless hand on Josh's shoulder. "That cub would be just about your size, sonny," he added, then walked into the night.

CHAPTER 3

No one talked after Thumbs left. One by one, they stood, yawned, and left the circle.

"Remember, buttermilk pancakes for breakfast," Lulu called as she walked toward the main house.

The kids stayed behind to help Jud douse the fire with pond water.

"Was there *really* a bear?" Josh asked Jud. "He was kidding, wasn't he?"

"I was away at college, so I don't know for sure," Jud said. "But I've never known Thumbs to be a kidder."

"It could be a true story," Ruth Rose said. "I read a book about grizzly bears once. The mother bears protect their young until they're all grown up."

Dink slung his arm around Josh's shoulders. "Don't worry, even a hungry bear wouldn't want you. You're too skinny."

"Want me to walk you kids back to your cabin?" Jud asked.

"Nope," Josh said. "I'm not afraid of any old bear. Besides, I bet Thumbs was fooling us. How did he really lose his thumb, Jud?"

Jud laughed. "You'll have to ask him," he said. "Sleep tight and don't let the critters bite!"

Dink, Josh, and Ruth Rose walked toward the three cabins. The stars cast a soft glow over the stones that lined the path.

Light came from Fiona's and Ed's

cabins, but the cabin in the middle was pitch-black.

"I thought I left a light on," Ruth Rose said.

"I thought you did, too," Dink told her.

"I *know* I did!" Ruth Rose said. Then she jumped on Josh's back and screamed, "THE GRIZZLY BEAR'S IN OUR CABIN!"

"Very funny, Ruth Rosebush," Josh said. "See if I protect you when the bear really comes!"

When they were all in their beds, Dink turned out the light next to his bunk. He rolled onto his side and gazed out the window.

Fireflies flickered everywhere.

Frogs and crickets made a sweet racket from the pond.

"Good night, you guys," Ruth Rose said from the other side of the room.

"Good night, Ruth Rose. Good night, grizzly bear," Dink said.

"I'm not speaking to either one of you," Josh said from the top bunk.

Dink smiled in his bunk. *Josh is so easy to scare,* he thought as he drifted off to sleep.

Suddenly, Dink was wide awake. He thought he'd heard something thump outside the cabin.

He sat up and peered through the window over Ruth Rose's bed. She was a sleeping lump under her blankets.

Dink didn't know what time it was, but he didn't think he'd been sleeping for long. Josh was snoring.

Maybe a pine cone fell on the porch, Dink said to himself. *Yeah, pine cones can make big thumps when they fall from tall trees.*

Dink lay back down and closed his eyes. He tried to force himself back to sleep.

Then he heard more noises. Something heavy was moving around on the porch, and it was no pine cone!

Suddenly, a dark shape stepped in front of the window. Dink shuddered and fell back on his pillow. Whatever was out there was large enough to shut out the starlight.

Dink heard a scraping noise, and then the shape moved away. Starlight once more flowed through the window.

Dink pulled his covers up under his chin. He could feel his heart thumping in his chest. *Calm down,* he told himself. *It couldn't be that lonely mother grizzly bear. Could it?*

Wishing he hadn't teased Josh about the bear, Dink finally went to sleep.

The next morning, the breakfast bell woke the kids. Josh leaped off the top bunk, nearly landing on Dink.

Ruth Rose dashed into the bathroom while the boys were getting dressed. Three minutes later, they were on the path to the main house.

"Um, guys," Dink said, "I know you're not gonna believe me, but something was on our porch last night."

"What kind of something?" Ruth Rose asked. "Did it have fur and big claws?"

"Here we go again," Josh muttered.

"Honest, something was out there," Dink continued. "I heard these thumps; then something blocked your window, Ruth Rose. There was a scratching noise, too."

Josh laughed. "You guys are so lame. It was probably a raccoon."

"If you're right, we'd better call *The Guinness Book of World Records*," Dink said. "Whatever stepped in front of that window was about six feet tall!"

"I don't care if Frankenstein was peeking in our window," Josh said, racing toward the main house. "I need pancakes!"

The kids hurried into the dining room. Everyone was already seated.

"Good morning," Ma Wheat said as she poured juice. "Hope you slept well and woke up hungry!"

Platters of scrambled eggs, sausages, and pancakes filled the middle of the table. Everyone dug in.

When most of the food was gone, Dink told everyone about the noises and the shape on their cabin porch.

"Strange noises?" Pa said. "I didn't hear anything. How 'bout you, Jud?"

"Nothin' could have woke me up, Pa," Jud said. "You hear anything, Ma?"

Ma shook her head. "You hear any strange noises, Thumbs?"

Thumbs grinned and shook his head. "Nope," he said, "but I thought I smelt bear when I walked over here this mornin'."

CHAPTER 4

Everyone had a good laugh—everyone except Josh. Then Pa asked Ed Getz to do a magic trick.

Ed stood up and showed his audience that his hands were empty. Next, he draped his napkin over one hand and mumbled a few magic words. When he yanked the napkin away, an egg was sitting in his hand.

Everybody clapped, and then Thumbs stood up. "Fine breakfast, Lulu," he said. "Those of you who want to, we're gonna pan for gold."

Twenty minutes later, all seven guests hiked with Thumbs and Jud along a gravel path on the other side of the pond. A stream followed the path, splashing and gurgling over rocks. Before leaving the main house, Jud had given everyone a wide, flat pan.

"This is it," Thumbs said a few minutes later, stopping at a sandy bank on the stream.

"I don't see any gold," Josh observed, peering into the water.

Jud laughed. "You won't see it," he said. He pointed farther upstream, toward the mountains.

"There's gold in those hills," he explained. "Every time it storms, nuggets get washed downstream. Show 'em how to find gold, Thumbs."

Thumbs squatted and dipped his pan into the water. "Don't step in the stream or you'll disturb the mud," he said. With a flick of his wrist, he brought up a panful of water and gravel.

"Gold is heavier than the gravel," Thumbs went on, "so it'll settle on the bottom of my pan."

Thumbs shook his pan gently back and forth, swishing the gravel and water. Then he tipped the pan and let the water and gravel slide over the edge.

"Lookee here," Thumbs said, holding his pan up. In the bottom lay a few dull pebbles. But among the pebbles was a shiny golden nugget the size of a pea.

"Is that *gold*?" Dink asked.

"Sure is," Thumbs said. He picked out the nugget and let everyone have a look at it.

"How much is it worth?" Josh asked.

Thumbs dropped the nugget into his

shirt pocket. "This size? Not much." He pointed his chin toward the distant hills. "To find the real gold, you'd have to go up there."

"Can we try panning now?" Ruth Rose asked.

Thumbs backed away from the stream. "Pick yourself a spot, and remember, don't get in the water."

The seven guests knelt along the stream.

Jud joined the kids and dipped his pan into the water. "I've been doing this since I was a kid," he said. "One year a

guest found a nugget the size of a golf ball. I heard he sold it and bought himself a new Jeep!"

"Cool!" Josh said. "I need a Jeep!" He knelt in the sand and dipped his pan into the water.

Everyone began dipping. For a while, all you could hear was the sound of gravel swishing against metal.

Dink soon got the hang of it. He liked the feel of the sun on his back as he dipped his pan over and over.

Suddenly, Fiona Nippit let out a

yell. "I found one!" she said. Grinning, she held up a gold nugget a bit larger than the one Thumbs had found.

"Great!" Jud said. "Now let's see if everyone else can find one."

Over the next half hour, others began to shout and hold up small nuggets, even Jud. Eight nuggets were found. Finally, only Josh hadn't brought up any gold from the stream.

"Gotta pack up soon," Thumbs announced. "Lulu's a bear if we're late for her meals."

"I'm gonna try a different place," Josh announced. "There are no more nuggets here."

"Where are you going?" Ruth Rose asked.

Josh pointed his pan upstream. "Up there," he said, "where the *real* gold is."

Dink watched Josh pick his way along the stream, tramping over rocks and branches.

"I hope he finds one," Ruth Rose said. "Otherwise, he'll be grumpy all week!"

Dink held his nugget up to the sun. It was the size of an M&M. "Do you suppose I can get enough money for this to buy a bike?" he asked.

Suddenly, they heard Josh yelling, then a big splash. They looked upstream and saw Josh sitting in the water!

Dink and Ruth Rose ran to help, but Jud reached him first. "Are you okay?" Jud asked, reaching for Josh's hand.

Josh grabbed Jud's hand and stumbled out of the stream. He was soaked from the waist down, but grinning.

"Look what I found!" Josh said, sticking out his other hand.

Dink's eyes bugged out. Josh was holding a chunk of gold the size of a potato.

CHAPTER 5

"Way to go, Josh!" Dink cried. He and Ruth Rose gave him a double high five while everyone else crowded around.

"That's the biggest nugget I've ever seen," Jud marveled.

The nugget was as large as Josh's hand and almost as flat. Particles of rock and dirt were embedded in the lump, but the rest was pure gold.

"Okay, folks," Thumbs said from behind the group. "It's time to get a move on."

Still congratulating Josh, the group

trekked back to the ranch. Josh's wet sneakers squished as he walked. Everyone headed to the main house for lunch.

Josh plunked his huge nugget on the table next to his plate.

"I bet I can make that disappear," Ed said, grinning.

"No thanks!" Josh said.

"You're a lucky boy," Pa told Josh. "But I wouldn't carry that around with you. You don't want to lose it!"

"Why don't you put it in our safe?" Jud asked. "Tomorrow we can take it to town and get it appraised."

"What's 'appraised' mean?" Josh asked.

"That's when an expert examines the gold and tells you its value," Jud explained. "Then you can sell it if you want."

"Okay, that'd be great," Josh said.

After lunch, the kids followed Jud to the office. The ranch office was small and dusty. Most of the floor space was taken up by a giant oak desk. A brown cowhide hung on one wall. Plants with tiny yellow blossoms were lined up on the windowsill.

Next to the desk stood an old black safe with a vase of dried flowers on top. As the kids watched, Jud hunkered down in front of the safe. He spun the combination lock back and forth a few times, then pulled the safe door open.

"There you go, Josh. Your gold will be safe in our safe," Jud said, grinning. He moved some papers and a green accounts book to make room.

Josh stepped forward and placed his nugget on top of the book. Then Jud slammed the door shut and twirled the lock.

"You all ready for that trail ride?" came a voice over Josh's shoulder. He turned to find Thumbs standing there with a toothpick sticking out one side of his mouth.

"Sure thing," Jud said. "Ready, kids?"

"I saddled the horses," Thumbs said as he left the office.

Fiona, Ed, and the Clydes followed Jud, Thumbs, and the kids to the barn.

Nine horses were saddled and tied to a corral rail. Each horse's name was stitched into its saddle blanket.

Pa and Ma pulled up in an old green truck. "Have a good ride!" Ma called. "We're going into town."

Everyone waved, and the truck raised dust as it pulled away.

"Can I have a nice gentle horse?" Dink asked.

Jud smiled. "All our horses are gentle," he said. "You can ride Trigger here. He really likes kids."

Trigger was pale gold with a white

mane. He looked at the crowd with mild brown eyes.

"Do you have any small horses?" Josh asked. "I'm afraid of animals that look down at me!"

"Barney is our smallest horse," Jud said. "He's a good ride, but he likes to stop and eat the wildflowers."

"Perfect for Josh!" Ruth Rose said.

Josh patted Barney's soft nose. "Be a good horse and I'll sneak you some dessert later," he said.

"Do you have any girl horses?" Ruth Rose asked Jud.

"Sure do," he said. "You can take Snowball. She's a real sweetie and has the softest gait in the bunch."

Snowball was fat and white with long eyelashes. She nickered when Ruth Rose rubbed her side.

Jud soon matched horses with Ed, Fiona, and the Clydes. "Okay, everyone, time to saddle up," he said, standing next to Bullet, a tall silver-colored horse. "Watch how I do it."

Holding the saddle horn with his left hand, Jud slid his left boot toe into Bullet's stirrup. Then he hoisted himself up and swung his right leg over the saddle. "Okay? Anyone need help?"

"I do!" Dink said.

Thumbs helped all three kids into their saddles and showed them how to hold the reins. He adjusted the stirrup straps to the length of their legs.

Just then Ed yelled, "Ouch!" He was half in and half out of his saddle. His right foot was hanging out of the stirrup in an awkward position.

Jud jumped off Bullet and ran over to help Ed get his foot untangled. "Are you all right?" he asked.

"I don't know," Ed said. He took a step, then winced. His face was white with pain. "That really hurts! I think I sprained something."

"You'd better get off that ankle," Fiona suggested. "Come on, I'll help you back to your cabin."

"No, you go ahead, Fiona," Ed said. "I'll be fine."

"Nonsense. I didn't really want to ride anyway," Fiona said. "I'll get some ice from Lulu."

With Ed limping beside her, Fiona walked slowly toward the cabins.

"Thumbs, would you mind staying behind to unsaddle Ed's and Fiona's horses?" Jud asked. "Then you can join us in the meadow."

Thumbs nodded and began unsaddling Fiona's horse.

"We'll ride in a line," Jud told the others. "Your horse will follow the one in front of him."

"Who goes first?" Josh asked.

"You do," Jud said. "Barney loves to lead the pack. Just touch his sides with your heels and he'll move."

Josh gently poked his heels into Barney's sides. "Okay, nice horsey," he said. "Giddyup!"

Barney shook his mane and turned his head to look at Josh. His ears twitched, but he didn't take a single step.

"Please?" Josh said.

Barney snorted, then started to walk briskly away from the barn.

"This is easy!" Josh called to Dink and Ruth Rose. "But you gotta say please!"

The other five horses fell in line behind him. Soon they were on a narrow trail surrounded by shrubbery and trees. The horses thudded over a wooden bridge that crossed a stream.

As the group moved through the trees, the ranch quickly disappeared.

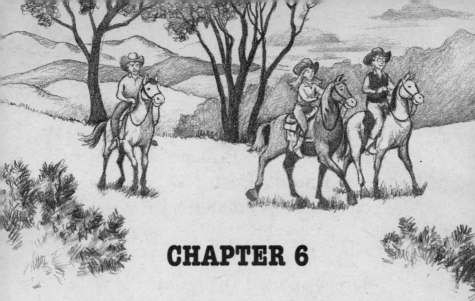

CHAPTER 6

The horses clip-clopped along in single file. Barney seemed to know where he was going, and the others followed. Jud, riding Bullet, was last in line.

Soon the riders entered a meadow. A blue pond nestled among the wildflowers. Josh's horse stopped under a pine tree and began nibbling a patch of weeds.

"We can let 'em graze here," Jud said. He helped the kids dismount, and the riders tied their horses where they could reach grass and shade.

"This is awesome," Josh said.

"Folks around here call it Paradise Meadow," Jud said. "There's fat trout in the pond if you'd like to feed them."

From his saddlebag pocket, he pulled a bag of bread crumbs from lunch. "Just sprinkle it on the surface and they'll come."

"Will you teach me to throw a lasso?" Josh asked Jud.

"Ask Thumbs when he gets here," Jud said. "He's the rope expert."

Jud tipped his head back and looked at the sky. A few dark clouds were mixed with white ones.

"There's rain coming," he said. "You'll find ponchos in your saddlebags, just in case. Storms come up pretty fast in these foothills."

"Can you identify any of these flowers?" Bonnie asked.

Jud grinned. "All of 'em. Tell you

what, I'll take whoever wants to on a little nature hike."

"We'd enjoy that," said Bonnie.

Jud looked at the kids. "You want to come along or wait here for Thumbs?"

"I want to feed the fish," Ruth Rose said.

"Me too," said Dink, reaching for the bag.

"Can I borrow your rope?" Josh asked. "Maybe I'll lasso a fish!"

Jud handed Josh his rope.

"Thumbs'll make you a rodeo star in no time," he said. "We won't be far off."

Jud, Seth, and Bonnie hiked toward the other end of the meadow. The kids walked to the edge of the pond. Dink yanked off his sneakers and waded in the water while Ruth Rose tossed crumbs. Almost immediately, trout gathered and gobbled them up.

"Watch this!" Josh said. He made a

loop in Jud's lasso and tossed it at a tree stump. The loop crumpled in midair and flopped to the ground.

"How do the cowboys do it?" Josh muttered, gathering in the rope to try again.

Just then hoofbeats sounded behind the kids. They turned to see Thumbs riding into the meadow on a big black horse.

"Hi, Thumbs," Dink and Ruth Rose said together.

Thumbs nodded but didn't answer. He dismounted and tied his horse near the others.

"Are you going to ask him to show you how to use that lasso?" Ruth Rose asked Josh.

"I don't know," he whispered. "There's something creepy about him."

"Don't be silly," Ruth Rose said. She walked over to Thumbs and said, "Josh wants you to show him how to throw a lasso."

Thumbs glanced behind her, where Josh was trying to coil the rope.

"I suspect maybe I can," Thumbs answered. His dark eyes swept the meadow. "Where's everyone at?"

"Jud took Mr. and Mrs. Clyde on a nature hike," Dink said.

Thumbs grunted. Then he walked over to Josh, took the rope, and quickly formed a large circle. He swung the loop over his head three times, then let it fly. The lasso whistled through the air and landed around the stump.

"How'd you do that?" Josh asked.

"It's all fingers and wrist," Thumbs said. He showed Josh how to hold the rope just as Jud and the Clydes appeared.

"Storm's moving in faster than I thought it would," Jud said. "We'd better head back to the ranch. Sorry to cut this short, folks."

Overhead, the few dark clouds had formed a wall of thunderheads. They were blowing out of the north, casting moving shadows over the meadow.

Within minutes they were all saddled up, wearing yellow hooded ponchos. Thumbs led this time, with Jud at the back of the line.

The sunny day had turned windy and cool. Sudden rain splattered through the trees. Dink felt and heard the drops as they splashed on his head and shoulders.

Thirty minutes later, seven wet horses carried their riders into the barn.

"I'll unsaddle Blackie for you," Jud told Thumbs. "Why don't you let Lulu know we're back so she can rustle us up some hot chocolate and cookies."

Thumbs jumped to the ground,

handed Blackie's reins to Jud, and jogged toward the main house.

The rain had almost stopped and a stiff wind was blowing the clouds past. Everyone dismounted and led the horses into the barn.

Suddenly, the dinner bell began to peal.

"Why's Lulu ringing now?" Jud said. "It's nowhere near suppertime."

When the clanging didn't stop, Jud ran toward the barn door.

CHAPTER 7

The Clydes and the three kids hurried after Jud. As they ran across the yard, the ranch truck pulled into the driveway.

Ma and Pa hopped out carrying bags of groceries. "What's going on?" Pa asked Jud.

"Someone rang the bell," Jud answered, leaping up the porch steps.

There was no one on the porch, but the bell was still swinging.

"Jud! Get in here!" Thumbs yelled

from inside the house. "I'm in the office."

Jud sprinted through the screen door, with everyone else following.

Nine people crowded into the small office. Thumbs was kneeling on the floor in front of Lulu, who was gagged and tied to a chair.

While Thumbs untied the knots, Ma removed the gag. Pa was already on the phone, calling the sheriff.

"What happened to you?" Ma asked.

"The safe!" Lulu cried, pointing.

The safe door was wide open, revealing a stack of papers and one green accounts book. The only thing missing was Josh's nugget.

"They got my gold!" Josh yelled.

"Can I have some water?" Lulu asked. She rubbed her wrists, which had red marks on them from the rope.

Bonnie ran to get water while Lulu told her story.

"I was in here watering the plants," she said, "when someone grabbed me and shoved me into this chair. I started to yell, so he gagged me, then tied me up."

"Who was it?" Pa asked. "Did you recognize him?"

Lulu shook her head. "He was dressed all in black, with a black hood over his face. Never said a word to me."

"Say, where are Fiona and Ed?" Jud asked. "They should've heard the bell like everyone else."

"Fiona made Ed lie down," Lulu said. "She wrapped his ankle, and I got him a pair of crutches. I offered to call a doc, but he said he'd take aspirin and be fine."

Jud ran out the door, and the kids followed. "Which cabin is Fiona's?" he asked over his shoulder.

"That one," Dink said, pointing to the cabin closest to the main house.

Jud thundered up the steps and banged on the door. "Fiona? It's Jud Wheat. Are you all right?"

When he heard no answer, Jud opened the door and stepped inside. "Oh my . . . someone go get Ma, quick!" Jud yelled over his shoulder. Ruth Rose barreled off the porch and raced toward the main house.

Dink peeked past Jud. Fiona was tied in a chair with a gag tied over her mouth, just like Lulu.

Dink grabbed Josh's arm. "Let's go check Ed!" he cried.

Dink and Josh ran to Ed's cabin. "Mr. Getz?" Dink called. "Are you okay?"

When no answer came, Dink opened the door. Ed Getz was lying on his bed. A scarf was covering his mouth. His hands were behind his back.

Dink untied the scarf and pulled it away.

"Thanks!" Ed said. "I thought I'd be here all day!"

He nodded toward his closet. "There's a gym bag in there. Look for a small box. Inside is a key. The guy used my own handcuffs on me!"

Josh found the key. When Ed sat up, Dink and Josh saw that his hands had been cuffed to the iron bed board. Josh used the key, and the handcuffs popped open.

"What happened?" Dink said. "They tied up Fiona and Lulu, too!"

"Yeah, and the rat stole my gold nugget!" Josh said.

Dink noticed that Ed's foot was tightly wrapped in a bandage. A pair of crutches was leaning against the bed.

"I was fooling around with my handcuffs, preparing to show you guys some tricks at dinner," Ed said. "All of a sudden, someone dressed in black burst in here. Before I could move, he cuffed me to the bed and tied this scarf around my face."

Ed shook his hands and rubbed his wrists. "Boy, those things were tight!"

"Can you walk?" Dink asked. "Pa called the sheriff. We should probably all meet in the office."

Ed propped himself up and stood on

his good foot. Josh handed Ed the crutches, which he slid under his arms. Holding his bandaged foot off the floor, he took a hop, then another.

"Let's go," Ed said. "Don't walk too close to me. If I fall, I don't want to land on you."

With Dink and Josh leading, the three of them moved down the path toward the main house. Up ahead, Ruth Rose, Ma Wheat, and Fiona were standing with a man on the porch.

In the driveway, a few chickens were pecking the tires on a green-and-white car. The word SHERIFF was printed on the door.

CHAPTER 8

Everyone crowded into the office.
While the sheriff took notes on a pad,
Lulu repeated her story. Fiona and Ed
broke in to add details.

"So the way I understand it," the
sheriff said, "some man or woman
dressed in black tied each of you up.
Then he or she opened the safe and
stole a hunk of gold. Is that about it?"

"Could it have been some stranger,
someone just passing through?" Ma
Wheat asked.

Lulu shook her head. "You can see a

mile in any direction from here, and believe me, I didn't see a soul."

"Maybe some passerby was hiding in the trees," Pa said. "It *had* to be a stranger—the robber sure couldn't be anyone in this room!"

Dink quickly glanced around the office. Everyone was doing the same thing, looking at everyone else.

"Lulu," Ma said, "did you happen to notice how this character got the safe open?"

"I couldn't see what he was doing," Lulu said. "He was crouched down with his back to me, but I did see that he was wearing gloves."

The sheriff walked over to the safe. "So we can't even get fingerprints. I assume the safe was locked. Who knows the combination?"

"Well, I do, of course," Pa said. "And Ma—Mrs. Wheat—and our son, Jud. That's it."

The sheriff thanked everyone and headed for the door. He handed Ma Wheat a card. "If any of you think of anything, please call my office."

The sheriff looked at Josh. "Sorry you lost your gold, son. I'll do my best to get it back for you."

Josh mumbled, "Thanks."

The kids followed the sheriff out of the main house. He waved good-bye and sped down the drive in his cruiser.

Everyone wandered back to their cabins in a daze. The kids sat down on their front porch.

"This crook was pretty clever," Ruth Rose said.

"What do you mean?" Josh asked. He formed a loop in his rope and aimed for the porch rail post. He missed.

"I mean the crook made it look like nobody on the ranch could be the robber," Ruth Rose said. "Seven of us were riding, right? So it couldn't be any of us. Lulu, Ed, and Fiona were tied up, so it couldn't be them, either. Ma and Pa went shopping and got back when we did. That's twelve people with good alibis. So who was the robber? Nobody's left!"

Josh sighed and coiled his rope.

"You're close, Ruth Rose," he said. "But you forgot one little thing. There were only six of us riding—us three, Seth and Bonnie, and Jud."

"What about Thumbs?" Dink asked. "He was with us—"

"OH MY GOSH!" Ruth Rose yelled. "Dink, Josh is right! Thumbs was with us at the end of the ride, but not at the beginning!"

Josh grinned. "Yep. He could've tied up Fiona and Ed after he unsaddled their horses. Then he did the same to Lulu, grabbed the gold, and hotfooted it up to the meadow."

"But Thumbs is practically one of the Wheat family," Dink said. "Why would he rob the ranch?"

"For the biggest hunk of gold he's ever seen," Josh said, tossing his loop at Dink's foot.

He missed.

CHAPTER 9

The kids sat and thought about Thumbs as the thief.

"I know you don't like Thumbs," Dink said to Josh, "but I can't believe he'd rob the Wheats. Besides, he didn't know the combination, remember?"

"Who says?" Josh asked. "If he worked here for years, he could've learned it without the Wheats knowing."

Dink picked up some pebbles and tossed them into the path. "Maybe it *was* some stranger," he said, "like Ma suggested."

"I keep thinking about them being tied up and gagged," Ruth Rose said. "Whoever did it was taking a real chance. What if we all came back from riding in the middle of it all?"

"That's another reason I think it was Thumbs," Josh said. "He knew we wouldn't be back for a while. And he knew Ma and Pa would be gone at least an hour. Have you guys noticed how he's always sneaking up behind people?"

"Guys," Dink said after a moment, "I wonder why the robber used ropes on Fiona and Lulu but he handcuffed Ed."

"Ed told us," Ruth Rose said. "He had the handcuffs out to practice some tricks. The robber saw the handcuffs and decided to use them."

"Maybe," Dink said.

"What, do you think Ed was the robber?" Josh asked, grinning. "I can just see him hobbling around, tying up people and cracking safes on crutches."

"Unless he was faking," Ruth Rose said.

"Faking what?" Josh asked.

Ruth Rose turned and stared at Dink and Josh. "What if Ed didn't really hurt his ankle? What if he pretended so he could stay here to rob the safe?"

"Ruth Rose, Ed was handcuffed and gagged," Josh commented. "He couldn't do that to himself, could he?"

"Well, he is a magician, isn't he?"

"Plus," Josh went on, "Fiona stayed with him. Unless you think she and Ed are partners in crime."

"Well, it's possible, isn't it?" Ruth Rose asked.

"I guess it could be any of them," Dink said. "But how do we prove it?"

"I still say it was Thumbs," Josh said after a minute. "He knows a lot about ropes, and I bet he wore gloves so no one would see his missing thumb."

"Josh, a lot of people know how to tie knots," Dink said, "and anyone planning to rob a safe would wear gloves so he wouldn't leave finger-prints."

"Officer Fallon would say, 'Find the proof,'" Ruth Rose said. "So why don't we look in their cabins?"

"For what?" Dink asked.

"Clues," Ruth Rose said. "Like the black clothing this guy was wearing."

"And my gold!" Josh said. "Whoever took the nugget might've hidden it in his room."

"Wouldn't that be breaking and entering?" Dink asked.

"Just entering," Ruth Rose said. "All the doors are unlocked, so we wouldn't be breaking in."

Just then the dinner bell clanged.

Josh dropped his rope and stood up. "Let's go eat. My brain can't think when my stomach is empty."

They hurried to the dining room. While the adults talked about the robbery, the kids ate, kept quiet, and listened.

Dink looked around the table at the guests and staff. It seemed unbelievable that one of these people was probably guilty. How could that person sit here and pretend?

It can't be any of the Wheats or the Clydes, Dink reminded himself. *That leaves Ed, Fiona, Thumbs, and Lulu.*

Dink glanced at Ed, sitting on the other side of the table. His crutches were leaning against the wall. Ed was showing Fiona and Jud a trick using a piece of string.

Fiona was wearing a black turtleneck shirt over black jeans. Dink could see the red rope marks on her wrists. Was she the thief in black?

Lulu was bustling back and forth between the kitchen and dining room. Somehow, Dink couldn't picture her tying people up and cracking safes. But, like Thumbs, she might have learned the combination.

Dink looked down the table toward the seat Thumbs usually occupied.

His chair was empty!

Suddenly, Dink felt someone's foot kicking him under the table. It was Josh.

When Dink glared at him, Josh nodded toward the empty chair. Josh held up his thumb and wiggled his eyebrows.

"I *know* he's not here!" Dink whispered. "Cool it."

"What's going on?" Ruth Rose said.

Before Dink could answer, Josh asked Ma Wheat where Thumbs was. "He . . . he promised to teach me a rope trick after supper."

"Why, I don't know, Josh," Ma said. "Perhaps he's gone to town."

Pa tapped his spoon against his water glass. "It's been a bad day at the ranch," he said. "Why don't we all stay here after supper and play some cards? Ed, you can show us more of your magician tricks."

The adults at the table seemed to think Pa's idea was great.

Josh pulled Dink and Ruth Rose aside. "This is great!" he whispered. "We can check out the cabins while they're all here."

"But won't it seem weird if we just leave?" Ruth Rose asked.

Josh just winked, then walked off to talk to Ma Wheat. He came back a minute later. "It's all set," he said. "We're outta here."

"What did you tell her?" Dink asked.

"Just a little lie," Josh said, heading for the door.

Dink and Ruth Rose followed. "What kind of lie?" Ruth Rose asked on the front porch.

Josh headed down the path toward the cabins. "I told her we had a summer project we had to work on for school."

Dink laughed. "So what's the project?"

Josh glanced up at the sky. "Studying the constellations," he said.

"But we don't know anything about stars!" Ruth Rose said.

"I know that," Josh said. "But it's our cover. If anyone spots us running around in the dark, they'll think we're just stargazing!"

CHAPTER 10

"Which cabin should we do first?" Josh asked.

"I'll do Ed's," Dink said.

"I'll take Fiona's," Ruth Rose said. "Did you guys notice she was wearing black tonight?"

"Yeah, and Ed was doing knot tricks," Dink said. "Josh, why don't you check out Thumbs's cabin? It's out behind the barn. But be careful, he might be there!"

"No problem," Josh said. "I'll look for the truck and the station wagon. If one of them is gone, he's gone, too."

The kids separated and Dink crept up the steps of Ed's cabin. The wood creaked under his feet. Dink was nervous, even though he knew Ed was still in the main house.

He pushed open the screen door and stepped inside. The small light over Ed's bed was on.

Ed Getz wasn't very neat. Clothes were tossed around the room. A gym bag and duffel lay on the bed, half packed.

Dink quickly checked the dresser drawers. He found a book called *Magic Made Easy* and a few colored scarves. He also discovered a couple of pieces of rope, but they didn't look like the ones Fiona and Lulu had been tied with.

In the bathroom, Dink saw a bottle of aspirin, shaving stuff, and a purple toothbrush. A black rubber tube hung from the towel rack. At first, Dink didn't recognize it. Then he realized it was a stethoscope. *He probably uses it in a magic trick,* thought Dink.

Back in the main room, Dink checked the wall hooks. Shirts and pants were hanging there, but none of the clothing was black.

Dink felt guilty about poking around in some other person's room. But he wasn't hurting anything, and he wasn't stealing.

He peeked inside the duffel and gym bags. Each held clothing and a few books. Dink wondered why Ed hadn't finished unpacking.

Suddenly, Dink heard footsteps on the porch!

He froze, then dove behind the bed. He lay there praying the screen door wouldn't open.

Then Dink smiled. Of course! It was

Josh or Ruth Rose walking on their own cabin porch! The cabins were only about twenty feet apart, and the windows were all open.

Dink stood up and peeked out Ed's window. Josh and Ruth Rose were next door waving through the window!

Dink waved back, then hurried next door. "Boy, you guys scared me!" he said.

"What'd you find?" Josh asked him. Dink flopped on his bed. "A book about magic and some stuff to do tricks," Dink said. "No black clothing, and no gold. Sorry, Josh."

"Fiona has a lot of black clothes," Ruth Rose said. "And she has a ton of mystery books!"

"Anything about safecracking?" Dink asked.

"Nope, but I did check out that chair she was tied in," Ruth Rose said.

"I don't see how she could have tied herself. She could have done her feet, but her hands were tied behind her back!"

"She didn't tie herself," Josh said. "It was Thumbs. By the way, the station wagon is gone. I sure hope he didn't drive to town to sell my gold!"

"What's his cabin like?" Dink asked.

"Filled with stuff," Josh said. "My mother would love this guy, he's so neat! His bed was made and all his clothes were hung up."

"Josh, never mind how neat he is. Did you find any *clues*?" Ruth Rose asked.

Josh grinned. "Yup. He owns black gloves, black jeans, and a black ski mask! A bunch of ropes, too. And check this out—he has a TV and VCR, and guess what movie he's watching?"

Dink and Ruth Rose just stared at him.

"Famous Robberies of the West!" Josh said. "I saw the box it came in."

"That doesn't prove he's the robber," Dink said. "In fact, none of the stuff we saw proves anything."

"And we still don't know where my gold is," Josh said, coiling his lasso on his lap. "I was almost rich!"

Just then the kids heard a scuffling noise out front. They looked through their screen door and saw Ed hobble past the cabin on his crutches.

He moved slowly, holding his bandaged foot in the air. Once he made it up his front steps, he balanced on his good foot while he opened the door. Then he slipped inside.

"Josh, I know you're bummed out," Ruth Rose said. "I don't blame you. But maybe the sheriff will find the robber."

Josh shoved open the screen door and walked out onto the porch. He sat on the step with his lasso draped over

one knee. "By tomorrow, the guy will sell the gold," Josh muttered. "He'll get a bunch of money and take off and no one will ever catch him."

Dink and Ruth Rose joined Josh on the porch. It was growing dark, and fireflies were beginning to flicker in the bushes. Sounds of laughter came from the main house.

Dink sat next to Josh. "Want to walk down to the pond?" he suggested, trying to get Josh's mind off his lost gold.

Josh just shrugged and continued staring into the night.

"Okay, let's go," Ruth Rose said, "but let me get my bug spray."

She turned to go back in the cabin, then stopped. From where she was standing, she could see right into Ed's side window. "Guys, look," she said.

"What?" Dink asked, looking up from where he was sitting.

Dink and Josh joined Ruth Rose. They could see Ed Getz moving around the cabin, carrying stuff.

"What's he doing?" Dink asked.

"It looks like he's packing," Ruth Rose said. "Like he's getting ready to leave!"

CHAPTER 11

"Something's weird," Josh said. He tiptoed down off the porch and scooted over to the side of Ed's cabin. Dink and Ruth Rose followed him, and the three crouched under the window. They slowly raised their heads till they could see inside.

The gym bag and duffel bag were zipped and standing next to the door. The crutches were lying on the floor.

Ed was sitting on the bed, unwrapping his bandage. When the

bandage was in a pile on the rug, Ed pulled off his sock. He tipped it upside down, and out tumbled Josh's nugget.

"That rat!" Josh whispered.

Ed quickly jammed the nugget into his pocket. Then he walked toward the door. He wasn't limping at all!

"He's leaving," Dink whispered. "What should we do?"

"I'll go ring the bell," Ruth Rose said. "You guys stop him!"

Ruth Rose dashed toward the house.

"I've got an idea," Josh said, and ran behind Ed's cabin.

The cabin light went off, and Dink heard the front door open. He ducked down as Ed stepped onto the porch with his gym bag.

Ed looked around, then reached back through the doorway for the duffel bag. Carrying one bag in each hand, he stepped off the porch.

Suddenly, the dinner bell began to clang.

Ed Getz stopped in his tracks. At that moment, a rope loop fell over his shoulders. The rope tightened. Ed stumbled, then fell to the ground with a thud.

"Gotcha!" Josh yelled down from the cabin roof. He wrapped the other end of the rope around the chimney.

"What's goin' on out here?"

It was Pa and Jud, running down the path.

"I caught the crook!" Josh yelled from the roof. "My gold is in his pocket!"

* * *

The next morning, there was one empty seat at breakfast. Ed Getz had been taken to the Bozeman jailhouse, and Josh had his gold back.

"That sprained ankle was faked," Jud said. "After he knew the gold was in the safe, he pretended to be hurt so he could stay back at the ranch. I have a feeling he stole money out of my wallet, too."

"He must've gagged and handcuffed himself after he tied up Lulu and Fiona," Josh said.

"I'll bet he used that stethoscope to listen to the safe's lock and figure out the combination," Dink said.

"Seems that way," said Pa. He picked up a fax off the table. "This came in from the sheriff a while ago. Seems our Mr. Getz got himself into trouble in New York, too. He was a safecracker and a pickpocket."

"Hadn't been for these three kids," Jud said, "he'd have been long gone. There's a train out of Bozeman at midnight."

Thumbs looked down the long table at Josh. "You thought it was me, didn't you, sonny?"

Josh turned the color of the strawberries lying on top of his cereal. "I . . . we . . . how did you know?"

"I heard you three kids makin' your plans last night," Thumbs said. "I made myself scarce so's you could search my cabin. Then I just sat and waited to see what you'd find."

Just then they all heard a loud roar

from the kitchen. Before anyone could stand up, a fur-covered shape came running into the dining room, growling.

"What have you done with my baby bear?" it cried.

"Lulu, you'll scare these kids half to death!" Ma said.

Lulu stuck her head out from under the cowhide and grinned. "Hope I didn't frighten you too much the other night," she said.

"It was *you*!" Dink said.

"Yeah," she said, "but Thumbs put me up to it."

Thumbs winked. "Couldn't resist," he said.

Josh's huge nugget sat next to his cereal bowl, gleaming against the white tablecloth.

"That should bring in a tidy sum," Jud said, grinning at Josh. "I'll take you to town to sell it after breakfast."

"No thanks," Josh said. "I've decided to leave the gold here. I want you to sell it and use the money to save the ranch."

The table became so quiet all Dink could hear was his own heartbeat.

"Josh, are you sure?" Jud asked. "What about your new car?"

"Guess I'll just have to find another nugget," Josh said. He looked at Thumbs. "I'll show you my method."

Thumbs laughed. "I'm eager to learn, sonny."

"How can we ever repay you?" Ma asked Josh.

Josh just blushed.

"I know how," Ruth Rose said, giving Dink a little kick under the table. "Josh loves to be kissed!"

Ma stood up. "Well, that's easy," she said, heading down the table toward Josh.

"Me too!" Lulu said, puckering up her lips. She came at Josh from the other side of the table.

Josh charged out of the dining room, screaming as if a bear were after him.

About the Author

Ron Roy is the author of more than thirty-five books for children, including *A Thousand Pails of Water*, *Where's Buddy?*, and the award-winning *Whose Hat Is That?* When he's not writing a new story for the A to Z Mysteries® series, Ron spends time traveling all over the country and restoring his old Connecticut farmhouse.

Collect clues with Dink, Josh, and Ruth Rose in their next exciting adventure,

THE ORANGE OUTLAW

Suddenly, they heard a scream.

"Who was that?" Ruth Rose said, running back into the living room.

"It's my uncle," Dink said.

As the three kids ran down the hall, Dink peered into his uncle's bedroom. He wasn't there.

They kept running and practically bumped into him outside the little study. His face was white and he looked sick.

"Uncle Warren, what's the matter?" Dink asked.

"The . . . the painting," Dink's uncle stammered. "Someone's stolen Forest's painting!"